## Grayslake Area Public Library District
### Grayslake, Illinois

1. A fine will be charged on each book which is not returned when it is due.

2. All injuries to books beyond reasonable wear and all losses shall be made good to the satisfaction of the Librarian.

3. Each borrower is held responsible for all books drawn on his card and for all fines accruing on the same.

# Monster Boy at the Library

BY CARL EMERSON
ILLUSTRATED BY LON LEVIN

visit us at www.abdopublishing.com

Published by Magic Wagon, a division of the ABDO Publishing Group, 8000 West 78th Street, Edina, Minnesota 55439.
Copyright © 2009 by Abdo Consulting Group, Inc. International copyrights reserved in all countries. All rights reserved.
No part of this book may be reproduced in any form without written permission from the publisher.

Looking Glass Library™ is a trademark and logo of Magic Wagon.

Printed in the United States.

Text by Carl Emerson
Illustrations by Lon Levin
Edited by Patricia Stockland
Interior layout and design by Emily Love
Cover design by Emily Love

Library of Congress Cataloging-in-Publication Data

Emerson, Carl.
 Monster Boy at the library / by Carl Emerson ; illustrated by Lon Levin.
    p. cm. — (Monster boy)
 ISBN 978-1-60270-235-6
 [1. Monsters—Fiction. 2. Libraries—Fiction.] I. Levin, Lon, ill. II. Title.
 PZ7.E582Mo 2008
 [E]—dc22

                          2008003641

"Martha! Come quickly!" Mr. Onster called to his wife.

"What is it?" asked Mrs. Onster.

"It's Marty," Mr. Onster said. "You won't believe what he is doing."

Mr. and Mrs. Onster peered into the living room. There, Marty sat quietly reading in a comfy chair.

"Oh no," Mrs. Onster said. "Not again. He's acting like a . . . like a *child*."

The word made her skin uncrawl. For years, the Onsters had been hoping that Marty would start to act like a monster.

"Wait, Martha!" Mr. Onster said. "Just watch."

Just then, a tiny gopher scampered into the room.

Marty snatched it up. Then he gobbled it down whole.

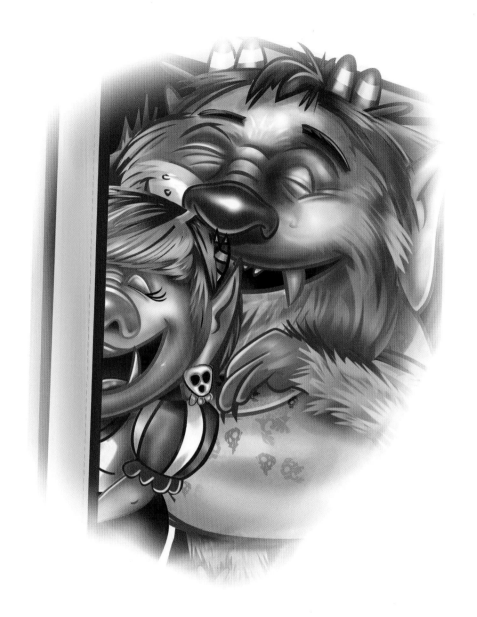

"Oh my!" Mrs. Onster yelped. "He's doing it!
Finally, he's eating creatures!"

As Mr. and Mrs. Onster hugged in the next room, they didn't see what happened next. Marty smiled broadly and the little gopher crawled in and out through the holes where he was missing teeth.

Then, he set the gopher back down on the floor.

"Have a nice day, Mr. Sprinkles," Marty whispered.
Mr. Sprinkles squeaked back at him and ran away.

Later that morning, Marty got ready for school. Mrs. Onster handed him his backpack.

"I've packed a nice lunch of hog bones and leech chips for you," Mrs. Onster said. "If anyone tries to take your food, you can bite their arm off."

"It would make a nice dessert!"
Mr. Onster howled, bits of food
flying everywhere.

Marty didn't laugh, however.
"Mom, Dad, you know I just
want to be like the other kids,"
he said. "Um, did you remember
to pack my snot rags?"

Marty raced to school. It was his favorite day of the week.
Every Tuesday, Marty's class got to have Library Time.

Each week the librarian, Miss Classified, read the children
a story and taught them about the library.

When the lessons were done,
the children could return the
books they had read and
check out new ones.

"I can't wait to read the next book in the Betsy Brash series," said Sally Weet, Marty's best friend.

"Yeah, and I'm going to check out Book 12 in the Max Platinum series," Marty said.

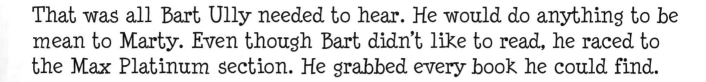

That was all Bart Ully needed to hear. He would do anything to be mean to Marty. Even though Bart didn't like to read, he raced to the Max Platinum section. He grabbed every book he could find.

Marty walked with Sally to the Betsy Brash shelf. "How about this one?" he asked, grabbing Book 7.

"That's perfect!" Sally replied. "I've been waiting for that one to be returned."

Sally and Marty walked together to the Max Platinum shelf. Marty couldn't believe what he saw when they got there.

"The shelf is completely empty!" he exclaimed.

Something began to change inside Marty. His belly felt like it was on fire. His skin felt like it was all gooey.

"Oh no," Sally said. "Not again. Calm down, Marty. It will be okay. Let's just ask Miss Classified if any Max Platinum books are behind the counter."

When they got to the counter, however, Marty could control himself no longer. There, Bart was checking out a pile of Max Platinum books.

"Hey, Monster," Bart said. "Uh, I mean, Onster. Looking for something?"

Marty's shoulders lurched forward. Everything inside him screamed, "EAT HIM!"

Marty tried to stay under control, but soon he was flying around the room. Marty bounced off the walls. He knocked over racks. He scattered periodicals. Reference materials tumbled to the ground.

When it was all over, the library was, well, disorganized.

"Sweet Dewey, what have you done?" Miss Classified cried.

As the anger disappeared, Marty became just a slimy, smelly mess.

Bart shook in fear. "Um, well, maybe I'll
just check out one of these," he said.

"Actually, we have a rule about series," Miss Classified said, trying to calm down. "You can only check out one book at a time from a series. That way, everyone gets a chance to read them."

"That sounds fair," Bart agreed, quickly picking up books from the floor.

Marty nodded. "That's a good rule, Miss Classified," he said, as he started to clean up his mess. "You should really post that on a wall."

"That's a lovely idea, Marty," Miss Classified said. "I'll have you make a poster during your next Library Time."

# Contain Your Inner Monster
## *Tips from Marty Onster*

- Take deep breaths and focus on each one to take your mind off of a situation that is frustrating you.

- Get all the facts before you react to a situation.

- Take a time out and step away from someone who is making you frustrated.

- Every day you control your temper, reward yourself with leech chips for a snack!